The Amazing Snowman Duel

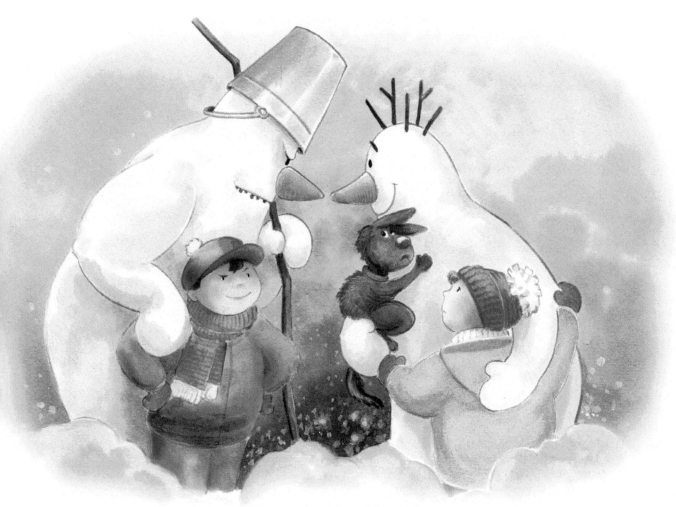

Written by Yossi Lapid
Illustrated by Joanna Pasek

ISBN 978-0-9973899-8-2

In loving memory of Marika.

I knew my friend Bill very well
And on that morning I could tell
That he was up to a new trick.
The new trick's name was

SNOWMAN NICK,

A giant snowman with a stick!

"Watch out!" said Bill. "Nick's here to fight.
He'll face-off with your Paul, tonight!"

"No way," I said. "That can't be fair!"

"Maybe," snapped Bill, "But I don't care.
Just know it's you who's backing out..."

"Oh, no!" said Paul. "We'll have this bout.
But I do hope you understand
That there are rules in Snowman Land."

"Whatever," laughed Bill, "but beware
At midnight Nick will meet you there!"

The Amazing Snowman Duel!

Word was out
About the bout.

They came by ground,

By sea,

The Amazing Snowman Duel

By air,

For Snowman Duels are quite rare.

Then, at midnight, a heavy rattle,
And there was Nick geared up for battle —
Helmet, armor, stick and all,
But there was no sign of Paul.

Guess where I found that sleepyhead?
Snoring happily in his bed!

"Paul," I yelled, "it's now midnight. Everything's ready for the fight!"

"Already?" yawned Paul. "Well, let's go;
Let's finish quickly with this show!"

And then Paul walked straight up to Nick
Without a helmet or a stick...

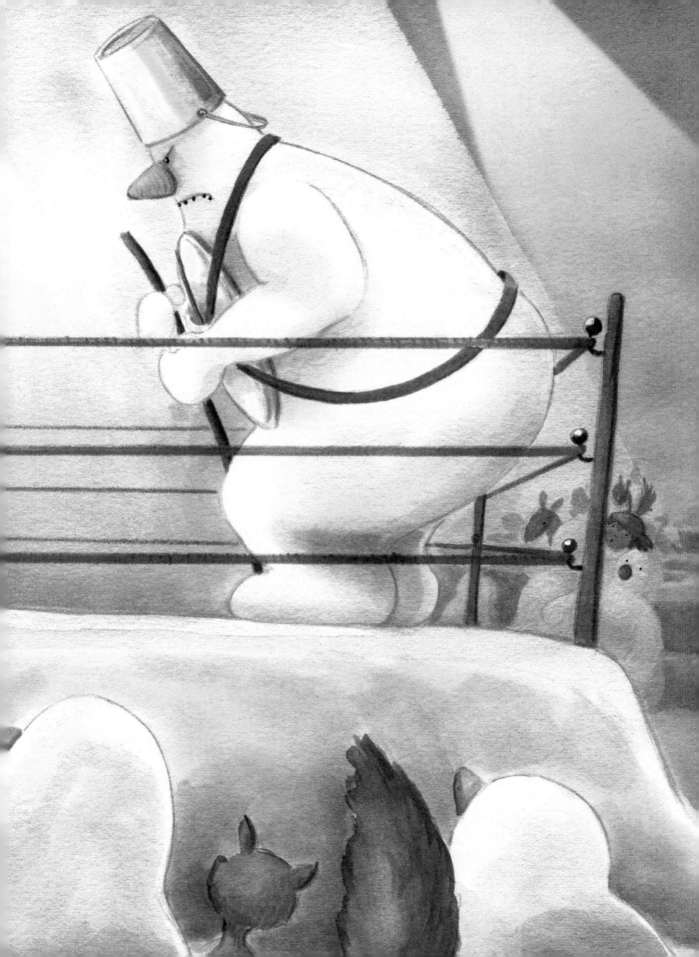

I put my hands over my eyes;
Is this the way my snowman dies?

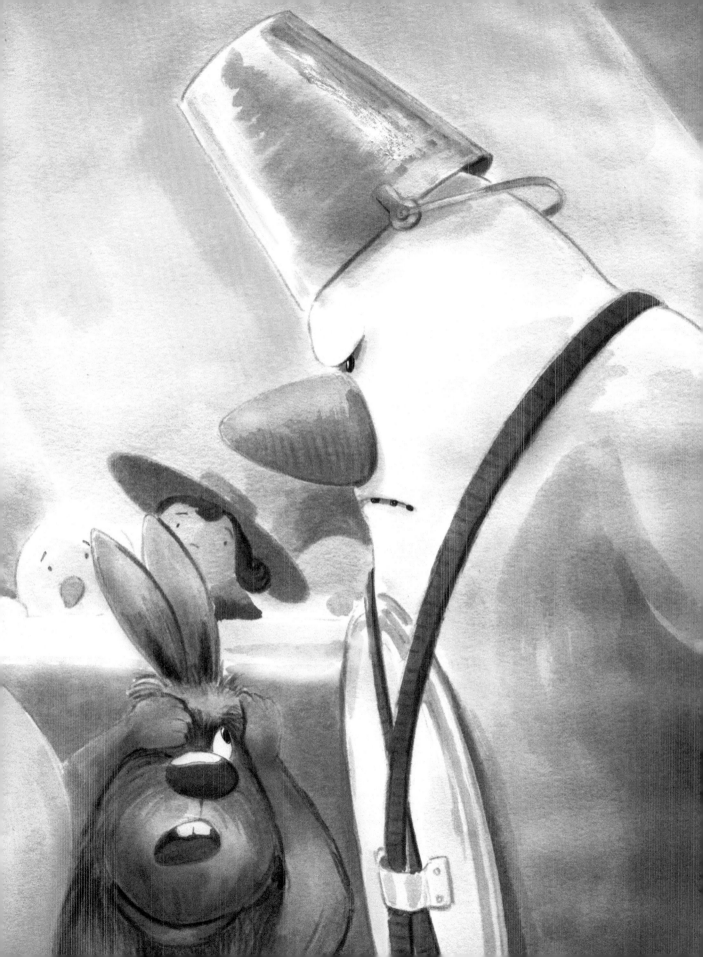

Then, I heard a sudden hush
And everyone left in a rush...

I wondered if the fight was done,
When Paul cried out: "Hey Dan, we won!"

"We did?" I gasped. "We won the bout?"

"Of course," said Paul, "I stared him out!
That's how it goes in Snowman Land,
We never ever lay a hand!"

"But tell me Paul, is Nick OK?"

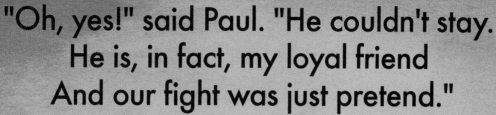

"Oh, yes!" said Paul. "He couldn't stay.
He is, in fact, my loyal friend
And our fight was just pretend."

"Awesome!" I said. "If Nick's all right,
Let's have a friendly snowball fight."

Then we sat down and drank together
Sweet hot cocoa, in chilly weather.

CPSIA information can be obtained
at www.ICGtesting.com
Printed in the USA
LVOW06s1509151117
556395LV00020B/271/P